MONSTERSAURUS

SAURUS

Claire Freedman and Ben Cort

SIMON AND SCHUSTER

London New York Sydney

With much love to Paul,
Jacquie, Liam and Nushy – **CF**

For Johnny and Anna,
with all my love – **BC**

SIMON AND SCHUSTER
First published in Great Britain in 2011
by Simon and Schuster UK Ltd.
1st Floor, 222 Gray's Inn Road, London WC1X 8HB.
A CBS Company.

Text copyright © 2011 Claire Freedman.
Illustrations copyright © 2011 Ben Cort.

ISBN: 978-1-84738-904-6
Printed in Italy
1 3 5 7 9 10 8 6 4 2

Monty **LOVES** inventing,

BUT things don't always work . . .

His walking toaster **RAN AWAY,** His robot went **BERSERK!**

One day Monty found a book:

INVENTIONS
VERY RARE!

CREATE YOURSELF A MONSTER FRIEND
BUT ONLY IF YOU
DARE!

The book said:

TAKE SOME BRIGHT GREEN SLIME,
A SOCK – PREFERABLY SMELLY,
HEAT TO A GOO WITH MOULDY CHEESE,
STIR IN SOME STRAWBERRY JELLY!

WHOOSH!

Bright sparks flashed,
Out shot a **THING** . . .

All swampy, green and wobbly.

"I'M BOGABLOB!"

the monster drooled.

Monty grabbed the book again:

TAKE SAWDUST – JUST A PUFF,
HEAT WITH A TIN OF OLD BAKED BEANS,
ADD BELLYBUTTON FLUFF.

"Pooh!" Monty gulped and held his nose.
"This mixture smells so weird!"

THEN . . . .

POOOOF!

An even crazier THING . . . .

A **DUST MONSTER** appeared!

"HEY, BOGABLOB!" Dust Monster roared, "Let's have a MONSTER FIGHT!"

"NO, STOP!" gasped Monty.
"WHERE'S MY BOOK?
I NEED TO PUT THINGS RIGHT!"

KAPOW!

went Monty's formula,

And from the fizzing mix . . .

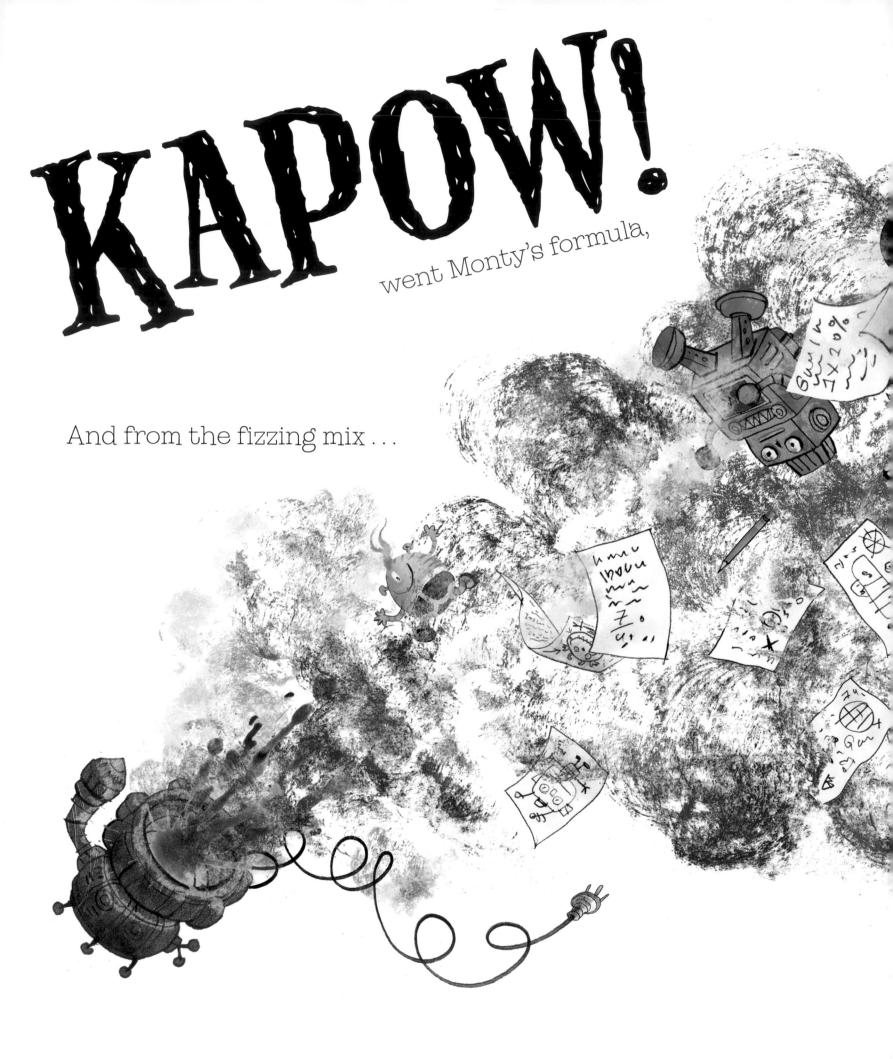

Burst big, bad **MONSTERSAURUS**

"I'll sort your monster fix!"

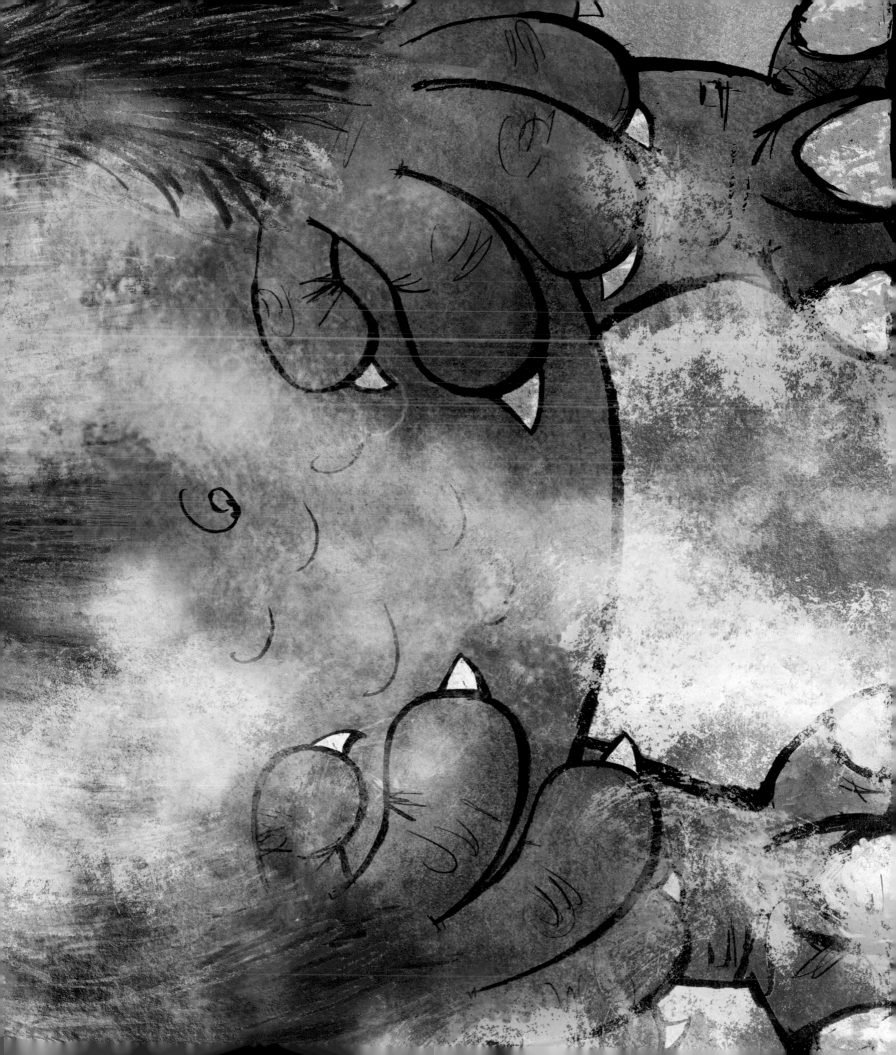

GRRRR!

Monstersaurus roared a **ROAR,**
And hissed a horrid **HISS.**

"Clear off, you measly monsters,
Or you'll get a **GREAT BIG ...**"

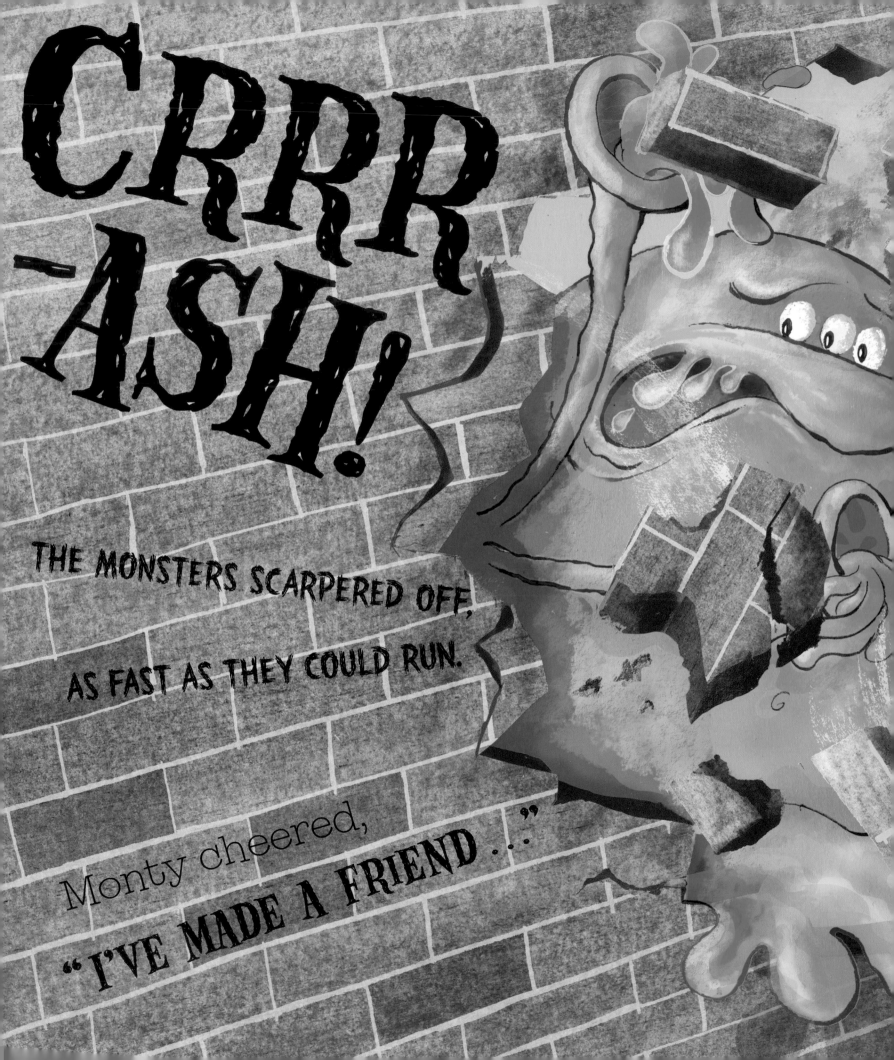

CRRR
-ASH!

THE MONSTERS SCARPERED OFF,

AS FAST AS THEY COULD RUN.

Monty cheered,

"I'VE MADE A FRIEND . . ."

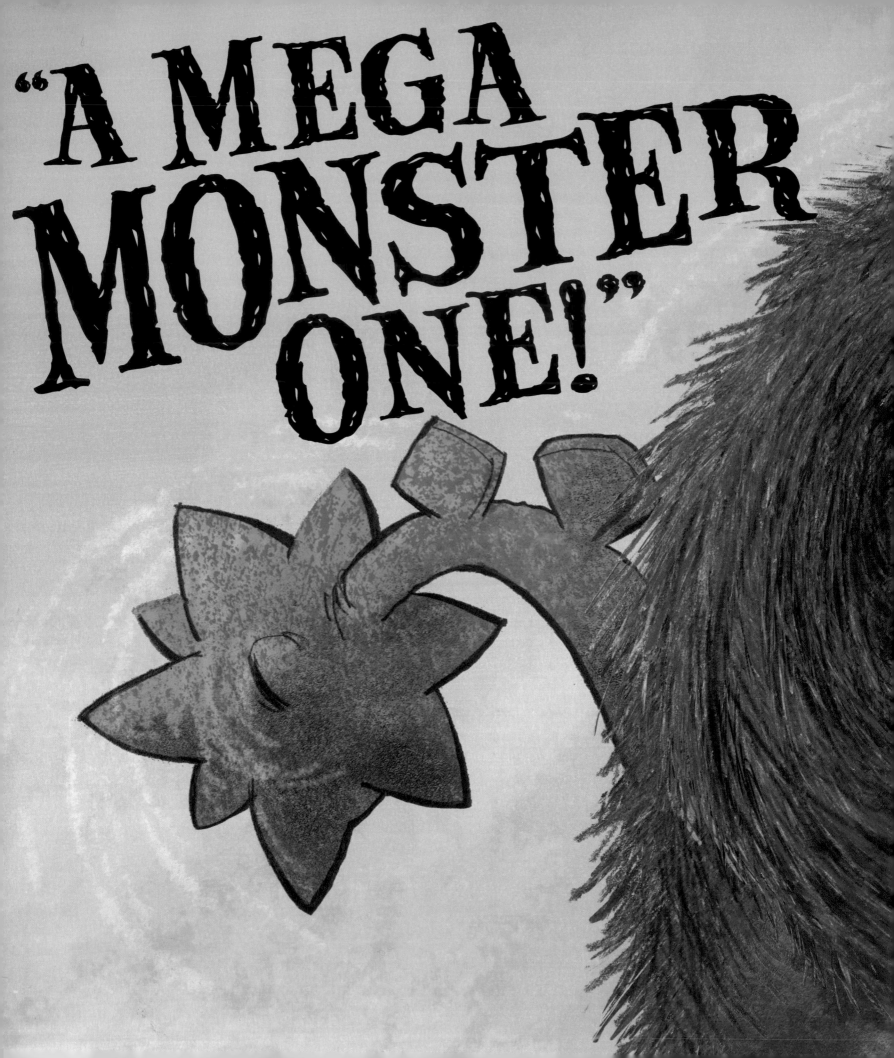

Said Monty to his new best friend,
"It's great - just you and me!"
What fun did they get up to?

YOU'LL HAVE TO WAIT AND SEE . . .